'Ingeniously-designed comic-cum-novel, a gothic pastiche that can be read as simple fun or as a literary lesson' *Guardian*

'Fast-moving narrative which has a wealth of strip-cartoons drawn in an amusing style to amplify it. . . Any youngster who likes ghostly tales of the macabre accompanied with much humour will get a lot of fun from this unusual book' *Junior Bookshelf*

'High melodrama, driven by anarchic, breathless plots . . . print is interspersed with illustrations-plus-speech-bubbles which you must read to stick with the story. . . Much care has gone into the physical design. . . Kids will love them, share them and return to them often to discover new things tucked away in the print and the pictures and the cracks in between' *The Times Educational Supplement*

D0190225

www.kidsatrandomhouse.co.uk/philippullman

OTHER BOOKS BY PHILIP PULLMAN:

His Dark Materials:
Northern Lights
The Subtle Knife
The Amber Spyglass

The Sally Lockhart books:
The Ruby in the Smoke
The Shadow in the North
The Tiger in the Well
The Tin Princess

The Broken Bridge
The Butterfly Tattoo
Mossycoat

The New Cut gang:
Thunderbolt's Waxwork
The Gas-Fitters' Ball

ALSO BY PHILIP PULLMAN
AND PUBLISHED BY DOUBLEDAY/CORGI BOOKS

Clockwork
Count Karlstein – the novel
I Was a Rat!
Puss in Boots (illustrated by Ian Beck)
Spring-Heeled Jack
The Firework Maker's Daughter
The Scarecrow and His Servant

NOW AVAILABLE FROM DAVID FICKLING BOOKS:

Lyra's Oxford

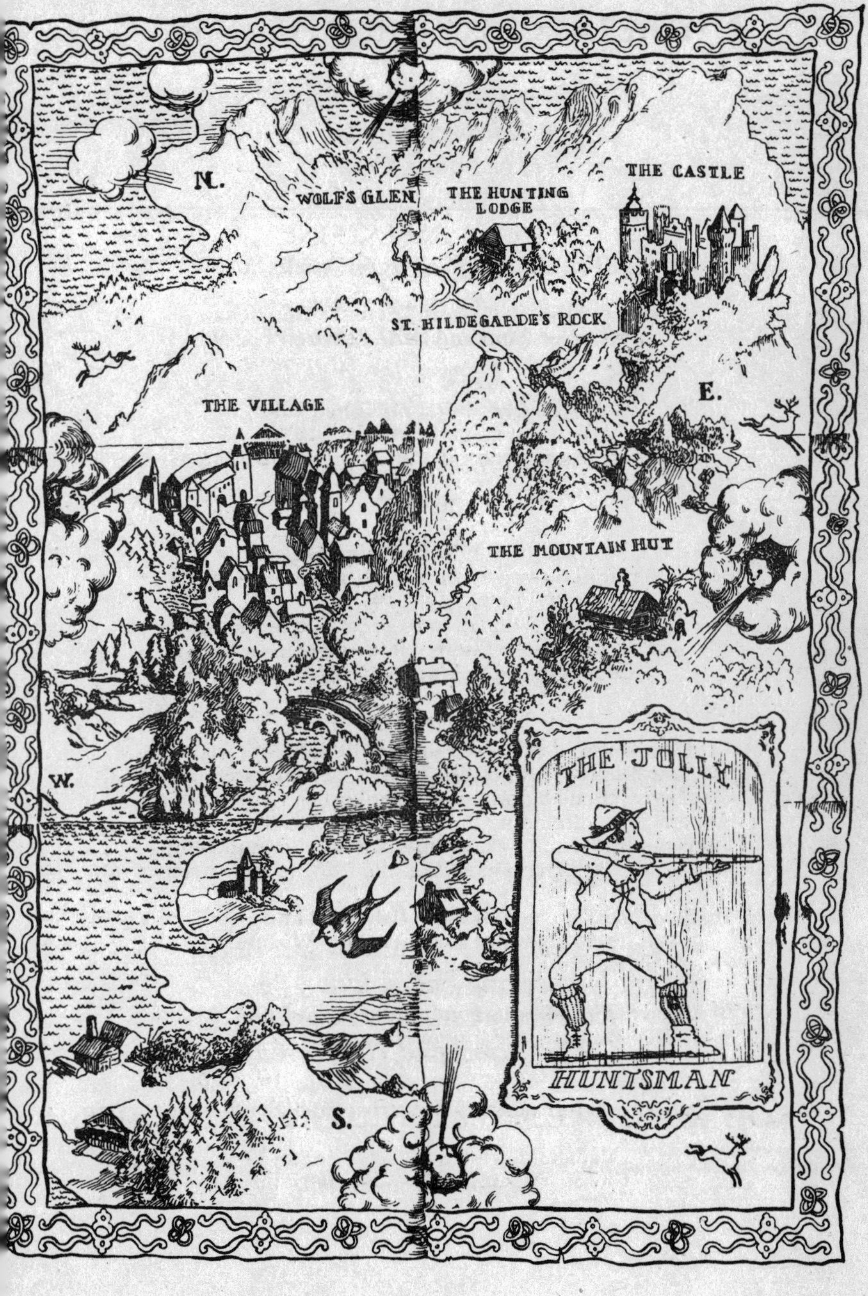
N.
WOLF'S GLEN
THE HUNTING LODGE
THE CASTLE
ST. HILDEGARDE'S ROCK
THE VILLAGE
E.
THE MOUNTAIN HUT
W.
THE JOLLY
HUNTSMAN
S.

COUNT KARLSTEIN
A CORGI YEARLING BOOK : 0 440 86266 3

First published in Great Britain by Doubleday,
a division of Random House Children's Books

PRINTING HISTORY
Doubleday edition published 1991
Yearling edition published 1992
Corgi Yearling second edition published 1998

9 10

Copyright © 1991 by Philip Pullman
Illustrations copyright © 1991 by Patrice Aggs

The right of Philip Pullman to be identified as the author of
this work has been asserted in accordance with the
Copyright, Designs and Patents Act 1988

Condition of Sale

This book is sold subject to the condition that it shall not,
by way of trade or otherwise, be lent, re-sold, hired out or
otherwise circulated without the publisher's prior consent
in any form of binding or cover other than that in which
it is published and without a similar condition including
this condition being imposed on the subsequent purchaser.

Corgi Yearling Books are published by Random House Children's Books,
61–63 Uxbridge Road, London W5 5SA,
a division of The Random House Group Ltd,
in Australia by Random House Australia (Pty) Ltd,
20 Alfred Street, Milsons Point, Sydney, NSW 2061, Australia,
in New Zealand by Random House New Zealand Ltd,
18 Poland Road, Glenfield, Auckland 10, New Zealand
and in South Africa by Random House (Pty) Ltd,
Endulini, 5a Jubilee Road, Parktown 2193, South Africa.

Made and printed in Great Britain by
Cox & Wyman Ltd, Reading, Berkshire.

COUNT KARLSTEIN

or THE RIDE OF
THE DEMON HUNTSMAN

PHILIP PULLMAN

Illustrated by Patrice Aggs

WITHDRAWN

CONTRA COSTA COUNTY LIBRARY

3 1901 04122 9123

CORGI YEARLING BOOKS

For Jamie again

CONTENTS

LIST OF

Heinrich Müller (later to be Count Karlstein)

Count Karlstein

Charlotte and Lucy, nieces of Count Karlstein

Zamiel, the Demon Huntsman

Dr Cadaverezzi, an Italian showman

Max Grindoff, once a coachman, now
Dr Cadaverezzi's servant

Miss Augusta Davenport, a learned Englishwoman

Eliza, her servant

Arturo Snivelwurst, Count Karlstein's secretary

Sergeant Snitsch of the Karlstein Police

Constable Winkelburg, also of the Karlstein Police

Meister Hoffman, a lawyer

Hildi Kelmar, a maidservant

Peter Kelmar, Hildi's brother

Frau Kelmar, landlady of the Jolly Huntsman

The Burgomaster

CHARACTERS

Herr Pistlpacker, the referee of the shooting contest

Peasants (various)

A tree

A book (*Amelia, or The Phantom of the Vault*)

A suit of armour

A bear's head

A deer's head

A boar's head

A stag's head

Two elderly phantoms

The skull of Hans Pimpelheim

The portrait of an old lady

A wig-stand

An owl

A cuckoo clock

A bearskin rug

A gargoyle

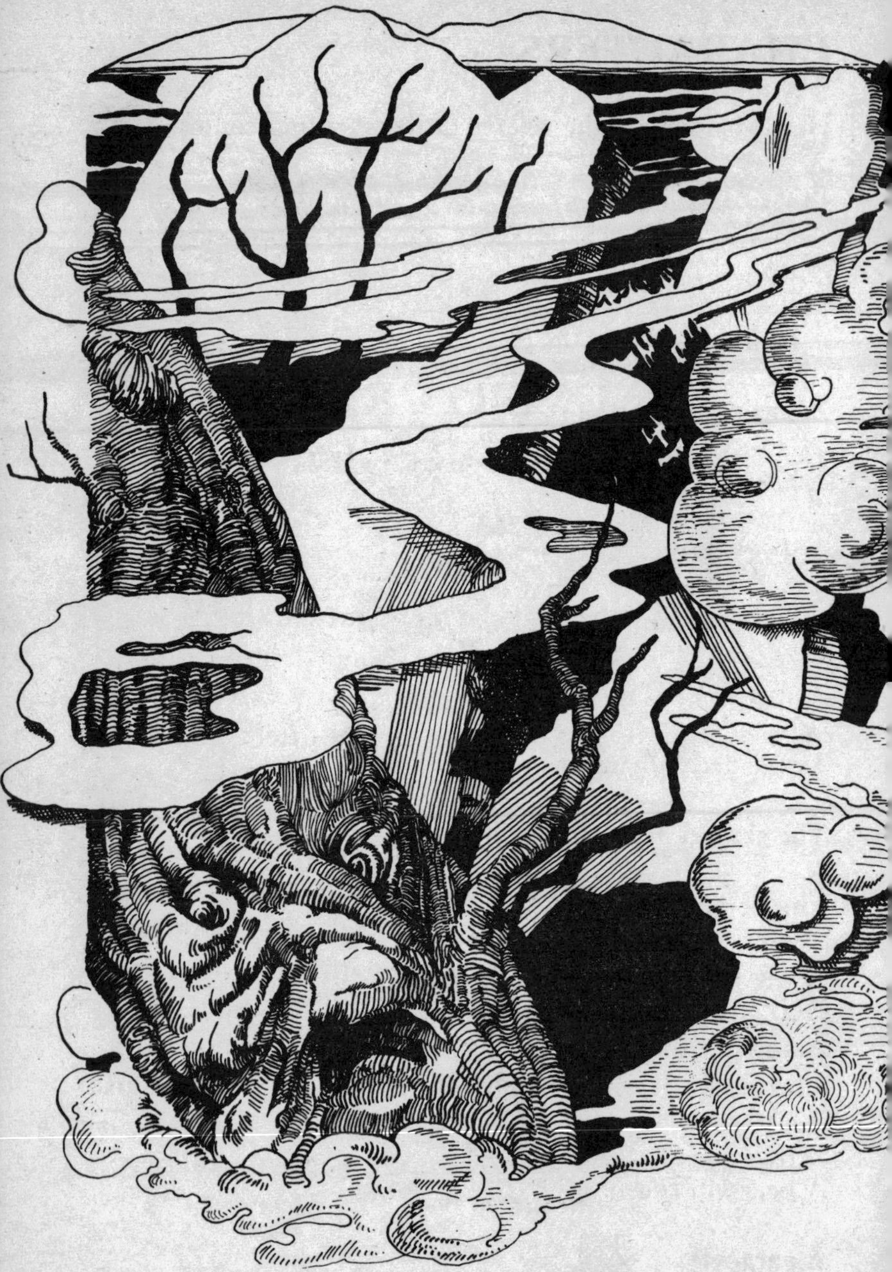

OVERTURE
The Wolf's Glen

In the depths of the deepest, darkest, gloomiest forest in the whole of Germany, there was a rocky little valley called the Wolf's Glen. And there Zamiel the Demon Huntsman, with his pack of ghostly hounds that filled the air with their howling, would come at midnight on All Souls' Eve to grant the wishes of any mortal foolish enough to make a bargain with him.

None of the hunters or woodcutters or forest rangers dared to go near the Wolf's Glen on All Souls' Eve. They stayed indoors with their pipes and their mugs of beer, and tried not to hear the terrible distant howling of the hounds, the faint echoes of a hunting horn, the far-off thunder of ghostly hooves in the sky.

But one year, someone did come to make a bargain with Zamiel . . .

The man looked up into the wild and stormy sky. Clouds were racing across the moon like a pack of hungry wolves. With trembling fingers he took out a hunting horn and blew a shivery blast.

The sound echoed around the bare rocks of the Wolf's Glen and was swept away in the gale.

Nothing happened.

Once again he set the horn to his lips and blew, and waited, and then blew it a third time . . .

And far away in the sky, there came an answering call: the sound of a wild hunt, with hoofbeats like thunder, and the baying of hounds like the cries of ghouls and goblins. The man shrank back with fear, and everything around the Wolf's Glen seemed to echo with the name of the Demon Huntsman . . .

And the Demon Huntsman laughed, setting the echoes rolling around the mountains and shaking the pine trees for miles around.

'Too late now!' he said. 'You have asked for a great estate and an honourable name, and that is what you shall have. For ten years.'

'Ten years?' said the man. 'And – what then?'

'Then you must bring me an offering. At midnight on All Souls' Eve in ten years' time, I shall expect a human creature, complete with soul, in the hunting lodge yonder. Bring that, and you can keep the estate and the wealth. Fail – and I shall have *you*, Heinrich Müller.'

The man gasped. 'How do you know my name?'

But there was no reply from Zamiel; only a terrifying laugh, and a wailing blast on a ghostly hunting horn.

And Heinrich Müller set off back through the forest, shivering but triumphant.

CHAPTER ONE
The Orphans, or The Deadly Oath

It was a winter evening. Down in the village of Karlstein, they were beginning to light the lamps in the houses around the square, and in the municipal hall, and in the Jolly Huntsman. Up on the great grim mountain, the last of the sunlight glowed on the windows of Castle Karlstein.

Out in the forest, the snow gleamed with a ghostly glimmer on the ground and on the branches of the millions of pine trees. There were no lights in the forest rangers' huts, no lights in the hunting lodge near the Wolf's Glen, no lights in the farmhouses high up on the Alps where the cows pastured during the summer.

Outside the police station, Sergeant Snitsch was putting up a poster.

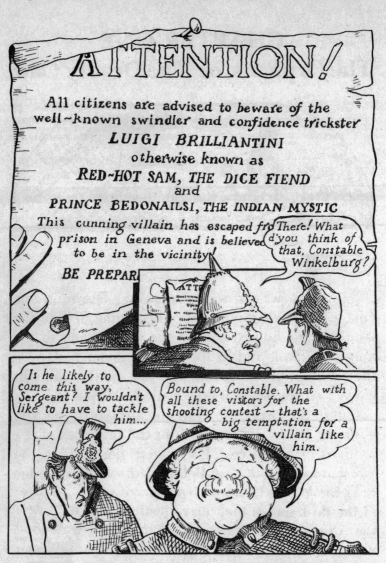

It was no ordinary shooting contest. There was a vacancy in the ranks of the Forest Rangers, and whoever won the contest would have the right to put on the green uniform and take charge of every living thing in the forest, whether it grew in the ground, or ran over it, or flew through the air above it.

The village was full of men from far and wide, eager to prove their skill, polishing their muskets and practising their shooting all day long, and guzzling and drinking in the Jolly Huntsman every evening. However, one traveller obviously hadn't come to stay. His coach rattled through the village, splashing Sergeant Snitsch, and then took the forest road up to Castle Karlstein.

The castle was a handsome building, from a distance. It wasn't so nice inside, though. There were rats behind the mouldy tapestries, with long sharp yellow teeth and dirty habits, and if you listened carefully you could hear a million wood-worms licking their little lips. The place was a mess, in other words.

As the sun went down that evening, two young girls were sitting in a window-seat to catch the last of the light, reading a book called *Amelia, or The Phantom of the Vault.*

Lucy and Charlotte were orphans. They had been living at Castle Karlstein for a year now, with their uncle the Count, who hadn't wanted nieces to look after at all. But he had had to take them in, because their parents had been drowned in a shipwreck and they had nowhere else to go.

19

They crept downstairs to the drawing-room, and pressed their ears to the door.

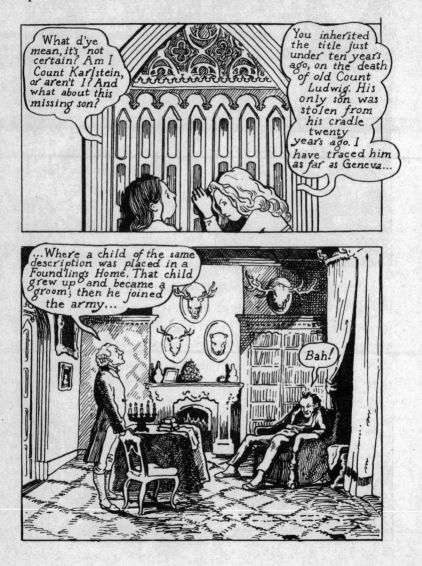

Suddenly Count Karlstein snatched open the door. In tumbled the two girls.

'Prying, eh?' he snarled, but he didn't hit them, because the lawyer was watching.

'No, Uncle Heinrich!' said Charlotte.

'We saw Meister Hoffman arrive and – and we came down to pay our respects,' said Lucy.

The old lawyer shook their hands politely, and Count Karlstein grumpily poured out some wine.

The girls were astonished. A holiday? They couldn't imagine anything more surprising. But as soon as the lawyer had gone, Count Karlstein told them more about it.

'We're going to my hunting lodge,' he said. 'Tomorrow afternoon. Just for a few days. Won't that be fun?'

The girls' hearts sank.

'Thank you, Uncle Heinrich,' said Lucy.

'That would be very pleasant,' said Charlotte.

'Good. That's settled then. Off you go,' he said, smiling wolfishly.

The girls didn't like hunting at the best of times, and the idea of struggling through the snow to watch Count Karlstein hack the life out of some poor deer, and then spending the evening twiddling their thumbs while he got drunk with his chief huntsman, didn't appeal at all. But they were too well-behaved to protest, and they went back to their room and *Amelia, or The Phantom of the Vault*.

22

Later that evening, Count Karlstein was talking to his secretary, who was called Arturo Snivelwurst. What they didn't know was that the maidservant Hildi was outside the room, polishing a suit of armour.

She never listened at doors as a rule, but when she heard a certain word, she nearly dropped the Shine-O.

Hildi listened, horrified. Then she ran up to the girls' bedroom.

Lucy and Charlotte had never heard of Zamiel. But when Hildi explained, their blood ran cold.

'The Demon Huntsman?' said Lucy faintly.

'But it's worse than that, miss! Your uncle made a bargain with the Demon Huntsman, and when you go up to the hunting lodge tomorrow afternoon, he's going to leave you up there *as a sacrifice . . .*'

The girls gaped. Nothing they'd read in *Rudolph, or The Hermit of the Forest*, or *Verezzi, or The Poisoned Chalice*, or *Montoni the Vampyre, or The Cup of Blood* had been anywhere near as frightening.

As they stared out at the stormy sky, they seemed to hear the baying of phantom hounds, the wild sound of a hunting horn.

'What can we *do*?' said Charlotte.

'We can't go anywhere tonight,' said Hildi. 'It's too wild – you'd perish of cold. I'd take you down to the Jolly Huntsman – my mum's the landlady – but it's so crowded, and they're bound to look there . . . I know! The mountain hut! We'll go there first thing in the morning.'

'A mountain hut?' said Lucy faintly. 'Not too close to a precipice, I hope?'

'It's quite safe! My brother Peter shelters there when he's hunting. Only he's in hiding too at the moment, 'cause they're after him for poaching – only he never – but Count Karlstein swears he did – and now he can't enter the shooting contest, 'cause he'd be arrested —'

'Never mind that,' said Hildi. 'Get your warmest clothes packed and ready. First thing in the morning!'

Lucy and Charlotte did as she said. They didn't have many clothes anyway, so it only took thirty seconds. Then they sat staring out of the window, not daring to go to sleep, while the wind howled among the battlements and the snow fell thickly all around.

CHAPTER TWO
The Bluestocking, or
The Secret Agent

Next morning, while Hildi and the girls crept away from the castle and made for the mountain hut, the Jolly Huntsman was filling up with guests. Most of them had come for the shooting contest, but there were a couple who hadn't.

These were Miss Augusta Davenport and her maid, Eliza.

'Lor, it's cold, miss,' said Eliza.

'You need not worry about that, Eliza,' said Miss Davenport encouragingly. 'Freezing does more good than harm. Travellers who freeze may be preserved intact for generations. Why, last season in London I saw a giant Siberian encased in a single unbroken block of ice in Signor Rolipolio's exhibition. He was complete to his very toenails.'

'You'd think they'd've thawed the poor man out, instead of staring at him,' said Eliza, trying to cope with all the luggage.

'I made that very suggestion to Signor Rolipolio,' said Miss Davenport, 'in the interests of natural philosophy. But he said that the shock of warmth would disenglobulate his cataplasm, and I dare say he was right. Now, where is the landlady? Ah! Frau Kelmar!'

29

Miss Davenport had been hoping to find someone to carry her portable laboratory up to the top of a nearby mountain. She wanted to test her theory that the glaciers were made of soda water. But if everyone was busy with the shooting contest, that might have to be postponed.

In any case, she had something else to do.

'Tell me, Frau Kelmar,' she said. 'Is the Castle of Karlstein very far from here?'

'An hour's walk up the mountain road,' said the landlady shortly.

'When I was Principal of the Academy for Advanced Young Ladies in Cheltenham,' Miss Davenport told her, 'I had two pupils who had to leave. Shipwreck – very sad. They came to live with their uncle the Count. I thought I would visit them.'

'Good luck to you, then,' said the landlady, leaving the room.

Sergeant Snitsch had decided that he'd better examine all the visitors, in case one of them was Luigi Brilliantini, the famous confidence trickster. So he and Constable Winkelburg had come down to the Jolly Huntsman, to carry out an inspection according to the rules laid down in the *Police Handbook*.

The Sergeant was very keen to catch this man. The only crime he had to deal with usually was poaching, but he'd never managed to catch anyone at it. He'd certainly never caught the landlady's son Peter, Hildi's brother, however hard he'd tried. But swindling and confidence trickery were much grander than poaching; he might even get a medal . . .

So that same morning, not long after Miss Davenport had arrived, Sergeant Snitsch came blustering into the Jolly Huntsman, with Constable Winkelburg trailing behind nervously.

But Miss Davenport had other ideas.

'I am not in the habit of standing in queues, Sergeant,' she said.

'Never mind, you're first anyway. Let's have a look at your passport.'

'I haven't got a passport, you ridiculous man,' said Miss Davenport. 'You don't require a passport to travel these days. The wars are over, and Napoleon is in exile. Do you take me for a spy?'

'There's no telling what you might be,' said the Sergeant, getting hot. 'I shall have to insist.'

'I beg your pardon!' said Miss Davenport. 'You are being remarkably impertinent. I shall show you nothing whatsoever.'

'You tell him, miss,' said Eliza. 'Pompous great pineapple.'

Sergeant Snitsch was flabbergasted.

'Take hold of my arm, Constable,' said Miss Davenport. 'Obey your superior officer's order, foolish though the man is.'

Constable Winkelburg took it, trembling. Eliza was dismayed.

In any case, I have been in worse situations that this. When I was exploring among the headhunters, the King of Borneo condemned me to death.

Wh-wh-what did you do?

I shot him. Rank is all very well, but I can't abide *foolishness*. Are you ready, Constable?

Constable Winkelburg certainly wasn't ready, but with the Sergeant's whiskers bristling at him, he had to go. Meanwhile, Sergeant Snitsch got on with inspecting people's papers, and very soon he found himself looking at a passport with all kinds of impressive stamps and seals and signatures on it.

'Dr Cad – Cadav – Cavara —' he read.

'Cadaverezzi,' said a smooth dark voice. 'Doctor of Philosophy at the University of Rio de Janeiro, and currently an agent of the Venetian Secret Service.'

A secret agent?

I imagine you are looking for Brilliantini?

Ah! You after him too?

35

Dr Cadaverezzi looked around. 'We must work together, Sergeant,' he said. 'There might be a medal for you if we trap the villain. But not a word to a soul!'

Sergeant Snitsch was deeply impressed. He could feel his chest swelling already with the medal gleaming on it. It could go next to his Neatness and Smart Turnout Award (2nd Class) from the Police Academy. He went on inspecting papers with more vigour than ever, while Dr Cadaverezzi pinned up a notice.

And with a last glance at Sergeant Snitsch, who saluted smartly and tapped the side of his nose, Dr Cadaverezzi sauntered up to his bedroom to prepare for the evening's entertainment.

CHAPTER THREE
Love, or Sausages

While all that was going on, Lucy and Charlotte were trying to reach the mountain hut. Hildi had written out some careful instructions . . .

How to Reach the MOUNTAIN HUT

Go up the ~~track~~ that leads from the stables as far as ~~THE~~ ~~Second~~ ~~third~~ SECOND Big rock on the ~~left~~ Right but not the Black rock, the grey one. Then there's another path going down between the cliff and where the bridge was Before it fell down. Further on there's Saint Hildegarde's ROCK but you won't see that because of the snow, so turn ~~right~~ left there and that PUTS you near the shrine. Turn up soon after that but Mind you don't take the fork that doubles back. ~~Go past the waterfall and up the side of the river~~ GO OVER THE FOOTBridge but Be CAREFUL because of the missing planks. When it's covered in SNOW you CAN'T see where the GAps are. Then the path ~~to~~ the mountain hut is STRAIGHT AHEAD OF you but it MIGHT NOT be very easy to see because OF the undergrowth. It starts on the Right of the ~~fifth~~ ~~sixth~~ fourth BIG tree — ignore the small ones — But they might be a Bit Bigger now

---

And so on. There were pages and pages of it. The poor girl had stayed up all night, and none of it was any use at all.

So within about ten minutes of leaving the castle, Lucy and Charlotte were lost.

But Charlotte wasn't having anything to do with caves.

'Remember what happened to Matilda, in *The Brigand's Cave, or The Fatal Marriage*?' she said.

Lucy shuddered. No, the cave wasn't a good idea.

'Perhaps if we followed the stream ...' said Charlotte.

'No! *Belinda, or The Skeleton Crew*!'

It was no good. Everywhere they looked seemed to be haunted by horrors out of the books they'd read.

'There's nothing for it,' said Charlotte. 'We'll just have to wander in the forest until we starve to death. I wish we'd never had to come here. I wish we'd never had to leave Miss Davenport's Academy in Cheltenham. I wish —'

'Remember what she said,' Lucy told her sternly. 'Young ladies should comport themselves with dignity even under the most trying circumstances.'

'Oh yes,' said Charlotte, unconvinced. 'I remember.'

They gathered their bundles, and wandered along the path, not knowing whether they were heading for safety or further into danger.

Meanwhile, something else was happening at the Jolly Huntsman.

When Constable Winkelburg had left with Miss Davenport, Eliza followed them. But she didn't get far, because there outside the inn was someone she knew.

Max was a coachman who'd driven Miss Davenport and Eliza about when they'd first arrived in Geneva six months before. He and Eliza had only known each other for a short while, but they were in love already, and going to be married, what's more. They'd last seen each other a month ago, but then Max had disappeared. Eliza had thought she'd never see him again.

Max told her what had happened. He'd gone into a tavern for a plate of sausages and some beer, and he'd put his musket down beside the chair. He always carried a musket on the coach, in case of highwaymen.

41

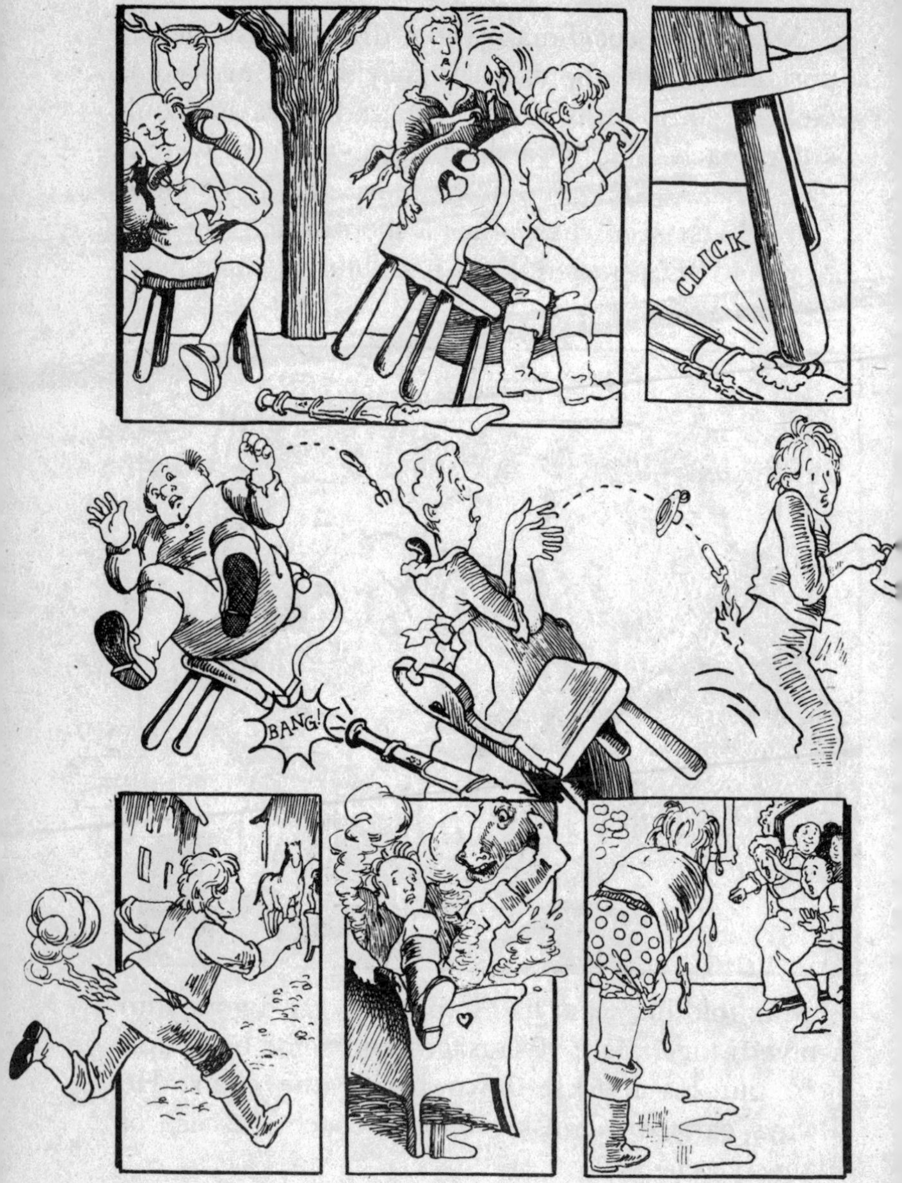
CLICK
BANG!

'See, they're very strict about britches in Geneva,'
he said, 'and mine was all burnt away. So they put
me in prison for a month. Luckily, I fell on me feet
there, though – I met Dr Cadaverezzi. When I was
let out, I found that he'd got out too, and he offered
me a job, being as I'd lost the coach. He's travelling
with this Cabinet of Wonders here, and he's giving
an exhibition of it tonight in the Jolly Huntsman. So
what d'you think of that, my little schnitzel?'

'Oh, Maxie,' she said, 'it's wonderful to see you,
only I'm so worried about Miss Davenport . . .'

She told him about Sergeant Snitsch. He shook his
head in sympathy.

'And I don't know how we're ever going to get
married!' she said. 'Everything seems to be going
wrong . . .'

'All right, my pumpkin,' he said. 'You still got that
little charm I gave you?'

He couldn't afford a ring, but he'd had a little
broken coin on a chain ever since he'd been a baby,
and he'd given that to Eliza instead.

''Course I have!' she said. 'That's my most pre-
cious possession, Maxie!'

They'd probably have stayed there all day gazing into each other's eyes if someone hadn't tapped Max on the shoulder.

Away went Herr Snivelwurst, looking for someone else to tempt. He had a nasty suspicion that if Count Karlstein didn't get Lucy and Charlotte back, it would be *him* in the hunting lodge, all trussed up for the Demon Huntsman.

As soon as Max had got the Cabinet of Wonders safely installed in the Jolly Huntsman, he and Eliza set off to look for the girls.

Meanwhile, Count Karlstein was in a fine old state.

Curse those girls! If I don't find them soon...

Yes? What d'you want?

A visitor, your Nobleness. A lady called Miss Davenport.

Davenport? Ah, yes ~ she had that wretched school in Cheltenheim or somewhere ~ Curses! What do I say to her?

Miss Davenport hadn't taken long to get away from Constable Winkelburg.

And since she wasn't allowed in the village, she'd walked up to the castle to say hello to the girls. She wasn't very impressed by Count Karlstein, though.

Will you have some brandy, Miss Davenport?

Thank you, no. I never touch alcohol, except in my patent "Promethean" winter boots.

Taken internally, it leads to hallucinations, convulsions, and rapid moral disintegration.

'I see,' said Count Karlstein, hastily swallowing his. 'And what leads to this visit, Miss Davenport?'

'I am making a scientific expedition,' she said, 'to test my theory about the pyramids. It is my firm belief, Count Karlstein, that the pyramids were built in ancient Britain and taken out to Egypt by the Romans. But on the way I intend to test my theory about the glaciers. It is an idea suggested to me by the great Signor Rolipolio. Frozen mineral water, you see, must contain an immense number of frozen bubbles. If the carbon dioxide in these bubbles could be extracted and bottled, think of the benefits! Where are the girls, Count Karlstein?'

Count Karlstein felt dizzy. 'The girls?'

'Lucy and Charlotte. I would like to see them.'

'Any other symptoms?' said the Count, mopping his brow. 'Why, yes. They are suffering from delusions. They imagine that I'm persecuting them. Ha, ha! How ridiculous. Ha, ha!'

'How extraordinary,' said Miss Davenport. 'I had better see them at once. I have studied medicine under Professor Wurmhohle of Heidelberg, and —'

'No! No!' said Count Karlstein in a panic. 'The doctor has absolutely forbidden any visitors!'

Miss Davenport looked at him hard, and then smiled sweetly.

'Then give them my regards, Count Karlstein,' she said. 'I shall be on my way.'

'Yes, I should,' said the Count. 'Best if you got away quickly. Good day, Miss Davenport . . .'

And he hustled her out.

Miss Davenport had explored all kinds of wild places, from Turkestan to Peru, so it didn't take her long to set up camp in a ruined graveyard by a rocky gorge.

Castle Karlstein

The Cliff

St. Hildegarde's Rock

Lucy and Charlotte's route

The Shrine

The Village

The Mountain Hut

N
W E
S

CHAPTER FOUR
The Egyptian Princess, or The Skull of Apollonius

Lucy and Charlotte were cold and tired and hungry. They were completely lost as well. And fed up. And frightened.

But worst of all, they were unlucky, because in spite of wandering about for hours and hours they'd hardly gone any distance at all.

They were so unlucky, in fact, that when they turned the next corner they saw —

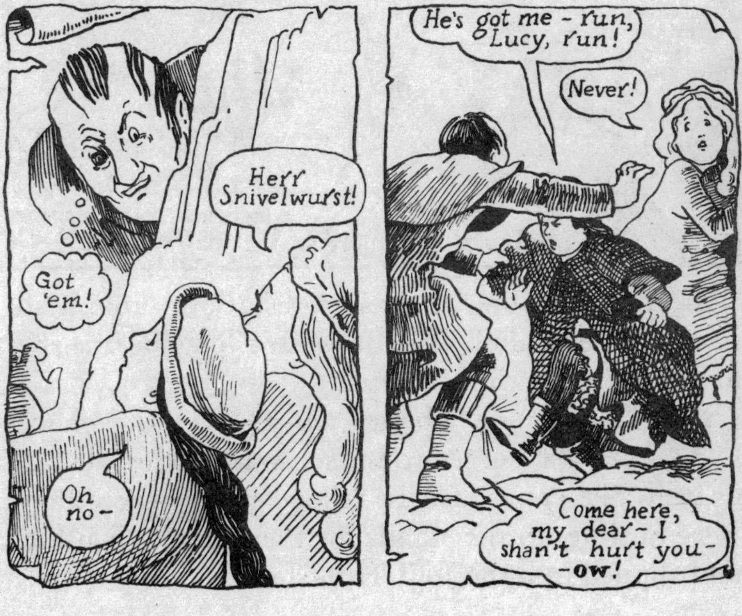

Got 'em!
Herr Snivelwurst!
Oh no –
He's got me – run, Lucy, run!
Never!
Come here, my dear – I shan't hurt you – ow!

They called him all the names they could think of, but it didn't make any difference. He had Charlotte in a firm and sweaty grip, and off he went towards the castle.

Herr Snivelwurst had taken Charlotte uphill, so Lucy ran downhill. And it wasn't long before she found herself in the village.

She thought she'd better not go near the police station, in case Sergeant Snitsch was looking for her as well. She crept past the village green, where they were putting up the stands for the shooting contest, and slipped into the Jolly Huntsman.

All the visiting marksmen were out practising with their muskets, so the place was nearly empty. But not quite, because in the parlour someone was calling.

Lucy did as Dr Cadaverezzi told her.

'But please,' she said, trying to look magnetic, 'I'm in terrible trouble. I must find Hildi —'

'Hush, child! You are standing on the edge of mysteries! In trouble, did you say?'

'Terrible danger – and my sister Charlotte's been caught – and – and will you not give me away?'

Dr Cadaverezzi was scandalized.

'But you are a vagabond, like me! A mountebank!' he said. 'I shall never betray a fellow-fugitive! They may wrench my body into splinters with red-hot tongs, but I shall never betray you!'

Lucy was very impressed. That was the sort of talk she understood.

'But will you help me get Charlotte away from the castle?' she asked.

'Of course. Now concentrate, please. You must be a princess – a magnetic princess.'

While Lucy was rehearsing her part as the magnetic princess, Charlotte was being imprisoned.

Herr Snivelwurst had dragged her all the way back to the castle, and found that the Count himself was out, looking for the girls somewhere in the forest, and getting more and more panicky in case he didn't find them. So Herr Snivelwurst decided to take charge, and locked Charlotte in a room at the top of the tower.

There was nothing out of the window but a hideous precipice, and nothing to climb down it with but a moth-eaten carpet. Charlotte sat down and gave way to despair. This was exactly what had happened in *Marianna, or The Sicilian Captive*, and when she thought of what had happened to Marianna later on, she nearly howled.

Then she thought of what was going to happen in the hunting lodge, and howled properly.

Meanwhile, in the forest . . .

But Miss Davenport hadn't had time to sort that 'out before someone else appeared, running down the forest path as if a pack of hounds was after her. It was Hildi.

She skidded to a halt and gasped, 'Miss Davenport?'

Miss Davenport blinked with surprise, but Hildi went on: 'I'm a maidservant in the castle, ma'am. I heard you talking to the Count – only I couldn't get away – and he's going to give 'em to the Demon Huntsman – and Lucy's lost – and they've got Charlotte again! They've locked her in the tower! Oh, ma'am, what can we do?'

'The Demon Huntsman?' said Max, gaping. 'By golly, they used to tell some tales about him, when I was a lad in the orphanage! He's got a pack of phantom hounds, and —'

'Don't, Maxie!' squealed Eliza, terrified.

'Eliza, control yourself,' said Miss Davenport. 'You have a practical nature (which is good), a warm heart (which is better), but a soft head (which is no good at all). There is only one thing to be done.'

'What's that, ma'am?'

'I shall have to go to Geneva.'

That puzzled them.

58

Then Miss Davenport surprised Hildi.

'I believe you have a brother,' she said. 'A huntsman, if I am not mistaken?'

'Why, yes, ma'am,' said Hildi. 'Only he's hiding from Sergeant Snitsch at the moment, on account of the Sergeant thinks he was poaching, only he wasn't.'

'Quite so. Well, take this to him,' said Miss Davenport, taking off a heavy silver bracelet. 'It was given to me by Signor Rolipolio, as a token of his esteem. We were going to be married, you know. But alas! He was unjustly imprisoned, and I never saw him again.'

'But what would Peter want with it?' said Hildi.

'He knows how to make bullets, doesn't he?' said Miss Davenport severely.

And then she left them. They didn't know what to make of that at all, but they thought they'd better do as she said. So Max and Eliza went up the track towards the castle, and Hildi went to the mountain hut (which was only five minutes' walk away) and found her brother Peter, practising his shooting.

Peter understood, even if no-one else did. He lit a fire and got out his bullet-making kit. Hildi watched, and the afternoon darkened as the storm-clouds gathered over the mountains.

It was All Souls' Eve.

CHAPTER FIVE
Show Business, or
The Prisoner in the Tower

It was evening, and the Jolly Huntsman was filling up with villagers and visitors, all eager to see Dr Cadaverezzi's show.

Lucy was sitting in the cabinet, hoping she could remember what she had to do, and hoping that Charlotte had managed to escape, and hoping that Dr Cadaverezzi would really help her after the show as he'd promised.

Just before they were going to begin, there was an interruption. The door opened and Count Karlstein himself came in, with Snivelwurst close behind him. Now that Charlotte was safely locked in the tower, he thought he'd come down and see the show. There'd still be time to take her up to the hunting lodge afterwards.

As the clock struck eight o'clock, a curtain was whisked aside, and there stood Dr Cadaverezzi.

'My lord, ladies and gentlemen!' he began. 'I, Dante Cadaverezzi, have exhibited my Cabinet of Wonders in all parts of the world. I was Honorary Physician to the Great Mogul of Tartary – I was Privy Councillor to King Alfonso of Brazil! And I bring before you tonight some examples of the curious and extraordinary phenomena I have discovered on my travels. For instance – this!'

He snapped his fingers. A little panel on the cabinet slid open, and out came a dark wrinkly little object. Dr Cadaverezzi took it carefully.

Dr Cadaverezzi waited until the man had opened it, and then said in tones of horror, 'No – don't open it! Ah – too late . . .'

'Too late?' said the man in alarm. 'Too late for what?'

'The very vapour of that dew is venomous in the extreme! It causes swift and agonizing torment, followed by boils, convulsions, gangrene, and . . . Oh, sir, you should not have opened it!'

'But what am I going to do?' said the man, in terror.

Everyone was watching, open-mouthed. Dr Cadaverezzi snapped his fingers again, and a little tray slid out of the cabinet.

Count Karlstein was beginning to annoy Dr

Cadaverezzi. Luckily, he knew how to deal with people who annoyed him.

'And now for an amusing trick with which I entertained the court of King Barmpot of Siam,' he said. 'Has anyone got a watch?'

'Here!' said Count Karlstein, holding up his gold pocket-watch. 'Take this one!'

The audience passed it up to Dr Cadaverezzi.

'I know what he's going to do,' Count Karlstein said loudly. 'He's going to pretend to smash it, and then find it somewhere else. It's an old trick. I've seen it before.'

People were looking around curiously. Dr Cadaverezzi wrapped the watch up in a big spotted handkerchief.

'And now,' he said, 'with your permission, my lord, I shall take this heavy hammer —'

'See! What did I tell you?' said Count Karlstein.

'— and smash the watch into pieces,' Dr Cadaverezzi finished.

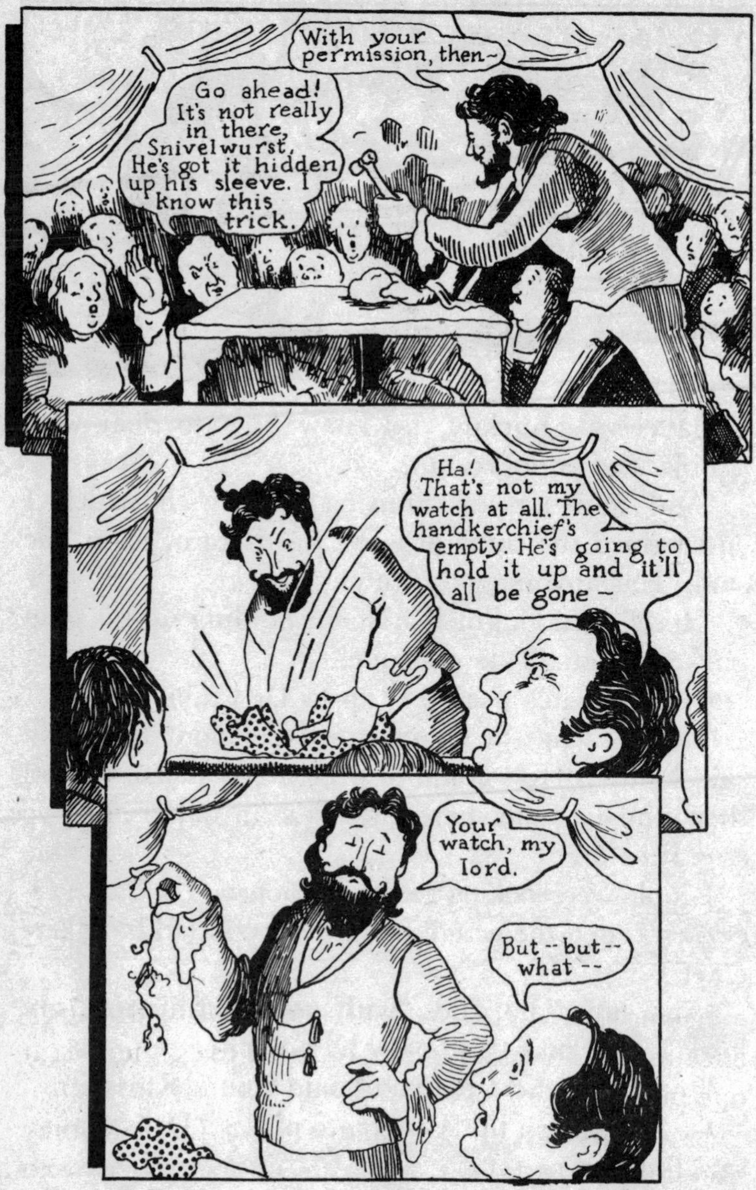

With your permission, then~
Go ahead! It's not really in there, Snivelwurst, He's got it hidden up his sleeve. I know this trick.
Ha! That's not my watch at all. The handkerchief's empty. He's going to hold it up and it'll all be gone ~
Your watch, my lord.
But -- but -- what --

Seeing Count Karlstein tricked had put the audience in a good mood. None of them liked the Count one bit.

'And now,' said Dr Cadaverezzi, 'for a display of etheric mentalism given by none other than the Princess Nephthys! She has slumbered in the pyramids for ten thousand years, but tonight she shall rise and speak to us in the hieroglyphics of her native tongue. Ladies and gentlemen – the Princess Nephthys!'

A puff of smoke came out of the cabinet, and a muffled gong sounded from deep inside it. The door slowly creaked open to reveal . . .

When she felt thoroughly magnetized, Lucy slowly opened her eyes and turned to face the audience. She was enjoying herself.

'O great Apollonius,' she began, 'reveal to us the mysteries of – AAAAGGHH!'

She'd seen Count Karlstein, only a few feet away. Then several things happened at once.

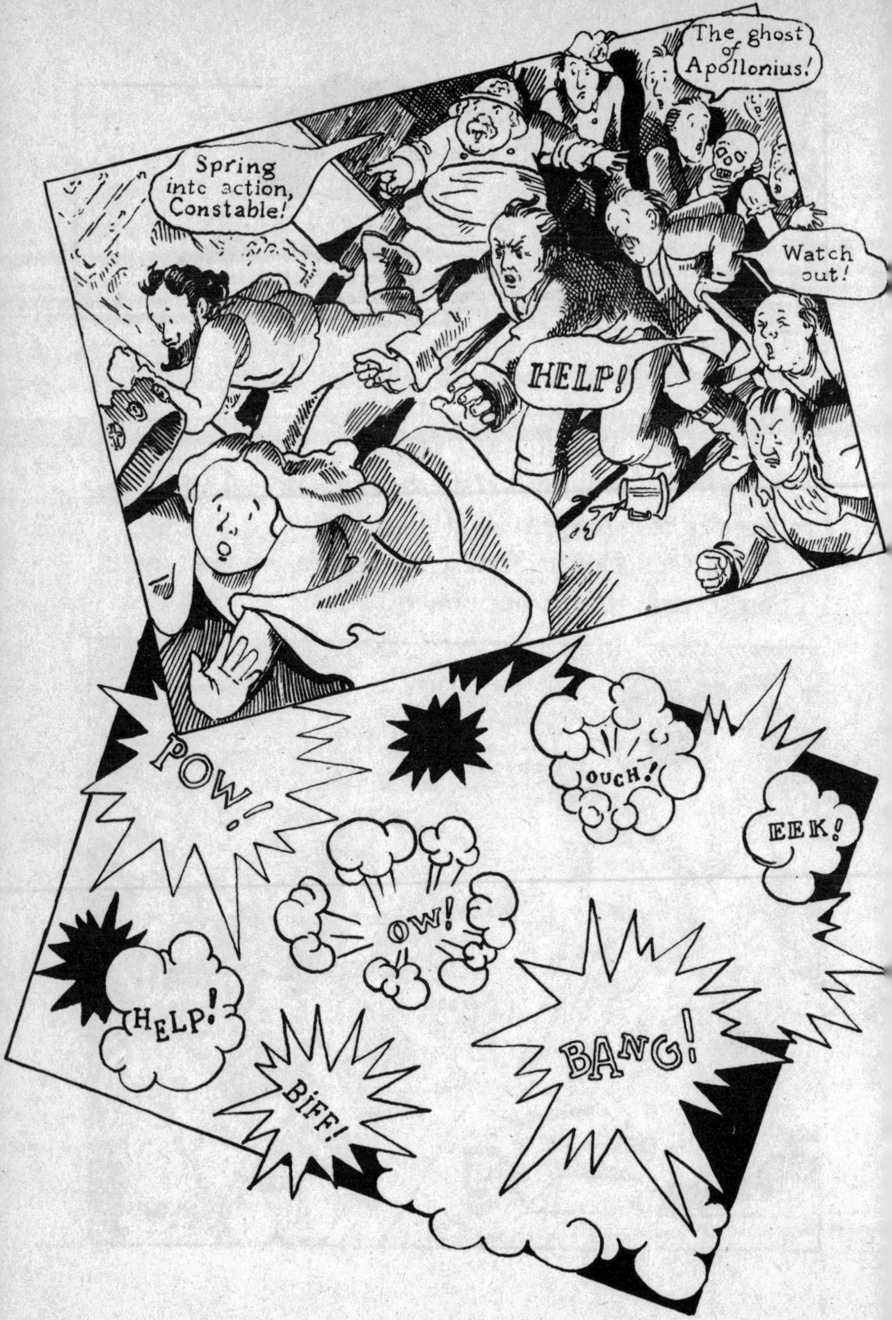
Spring into action, Constable!
The ghost of Apollonius!
Watch out!
HELP!
POW!
OUCH!
EEK!
OW!
HELP!
BIFF!
BANG!

Then the door opened, and everyone fell still.

Standing there holding a lantern was the majestic form of Inspector Hinkelbein, of the Geneva police. He was pointing at Dr Cadaverezzi, and a dozen more policemen were standing behind him.

'Luigi Brilliantini, you're under arrest!' he said. 'And where's that clown, Sergeant Snitsch?'

'Here, Inspector,' said an unhappy voice.

Sergeant Snitsch thought he'd better explain about Dr Cadaverezzi. 'He's not Brilliantini, Inspector,' he said. 'He's an agent of the Venetian Secret Service. He's called Dr Crackawhipsi, and —'

'Desist, buffoon!' roared the Inspector. 'And seize that wizard before he turns himself into smoke and pours out through the keyhole!'

71

The policemen rushed in and grabbed Dr Cadaverezzi. Sergeant Snitsch was using his police training to try and understand what was going on. Finally he worked it out. If Luigi Brilliantini and Dr Cadaverezzi were the same person, then one of them must be masquerading as the other, contrary to the law.

He was about to explain this to Inspector Hinkelbein, but the Inspector wouldn't listen.

'Take these idiots to a blacksmith and get them undone,' he told his men. 'Right, that's it, ladies and gentlemen, the show's over. I'm taking this cabinet into custody.'

And the customers settled down to their beer and their pipes and talked about what had happened, Count Karlstein and Snivelwurst climbed into the Count's coach, with Lucy held firmly between them.

All that time, Max had been busy trying to follow Miss Davenport's orders and rescue Charlotte from the tower.

While Eliza waited anxiously at the bottom, he climbed even more anxiously up. He wasn't very good at climbing, and he'd only got halfway when the Count's carriage rolled into the castle courtyard.

Maxie! Hurry!

You must be joking!

He scrambled up the ivy, dislodging owls and bats and creepy-crawlies, and he'd just reached the top when —'

Here - take this!

But who-

73

So there was another pair of Max's britches in ruins. He got down safely, but he was too late to stop the Count, and he and Eliza watched helplessly as the sledge swept out of the castle gate and up into the dark forest, towards the hunting lodge, and midnight, and Zamiel.

CHAPTER SIX
Midnight, or The Silver Bullet

*T*ick . . . *tock* . . . *tick* . . . *tock* . . .

The wheezy old clock in the hunting lodge was ticking like a death-watch beetle with rheumatism.

Moonlight filtered in through the dusty windows, gleaming in the long-dead eyes of the animals' heads on the wall.

Outside the windows, the pine trees clustered darkly.

Then she remembered the man at the window and the note he'd thrust into her hand.

Hastily she fumbled for it, and the two of them read it in the melancholy moonlight.

My dear Lucy and Charlotte,

No doubt you are alarmed to find yourselves in your present unhappy situation. However, do not despair. I have made arrangements for your safety, and everything will come out well.

Lucy, I do not have to see you to know that your hair is sadly disarranged. Charlotte, your stockings are wrinkled: they always are.

Tidy yourselves up at once. If you are to meet the Demon Huntsman, you should do so looking your best.

With kind regards from your good friend

Augusta Davenport

It's really her! No-one else would know that her name was Augusta!

And she's right. Your hair IS a mess.

Here! Look at me! Look at the time!

Charlotte - look - it's nearly midnight!

Victims... We're all victims...

He's coming! He's not far off now!

They'll never get away, you know. They're doomed!

As the girls sat there trembling, they heard a spine-curdling sound far off in the wild sky.

It was the ghostly wail of a hunting horn and the baying of hounds!

Lucy and Charlotte ran to the window and gazed out over the mountains. Clouds raced across the moon like small animals fleeing from the hunt.

They clung together, shivering with terror as the hideous sounds came gradually closer and closer.

Meanwhile, in the forest, four figures were stumbling over rocks and roots and fallen trees, trying to get to the hunting lodge before midnight. One of them had a great hole in his britches, but there were more important things than britches just then.

'How much further?' gasped Eliza.

'About another five minutes,' said Peter, who was leading the way.

Max was too busy scrambling out of holes and tripping over fallen branches to say anything, and Hildi was too anxious to want to. Besides, she'd just heard the same thing that the girls had heard, and she didn't want to listen too hard in case she heard it better.

'Come on, my little strudel,' said Max to Eliza. 'Take hold of me hand – that'll help.'

Eliza was glad to hold his hand, even though it meant that she fell in the holes with him.

'Ssssh!' said Peter, stopping on the crest of a slope.

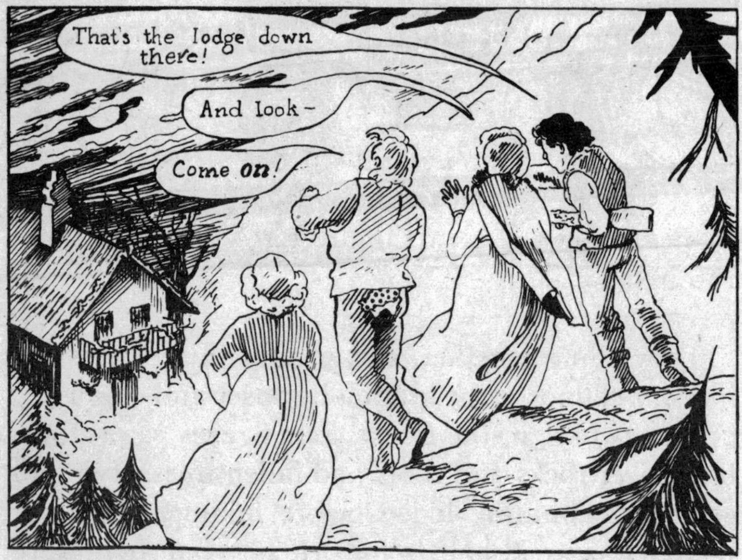

That's the lodge down there!
And look –
Come on!

They raced down the slope and banged on the door. But it was locked, and the girls inside couldn't find a key anywhere, and they couldn't open the windows either because they were barred . . .

'Hold this,' said Peter, handing Max his musket. 'I'm going to climb up that tree and across to the balcony and see if I can get in upstairs.'

As Peter scrambled up the tree, they could all hear the clock inside beginning to strike midnight. From somewhere high over the mountains, there came the sound of horses' hooves, and the baying of those terrible hounds.

Max looked at the lock, and then at the musket he was holding. He hadn't had much luck with muskets, but this time it might be different. He'd just had a brilliant idea.

'Stand back,' he said to Eliza and Hildi, and then called through the keyhole: 'Mind out the way!'

Peter, on the balcony above, saw what he was going to do and shouted, 'No! Don't!'

'It's all right!' Max called up. 'I learned this trick in prison. It's a good 'un. What you do is shoot through the lock —'

As the clock struck midnight they all ran up the slope and away from the hunting lodge.

The sounds of the wild hunt swept around them like a storm. And then —

And they watched as the wild hunt swept away over the forest and down the valley . . . towards the castle.

CHAPTER SEVEN
Retribution, or The Cuckoo Clock

Count Karlstein poured himself a large glass of brandy and Snivelwurst a small one.

'Success!' he said, as the glasses clinked together.

They were in Count Karlstein's study at the top of the highest tower in the castle. They'd just got back from the hunting lodge. The horses were being washed and polished by the groom, and there was nothing to do now but have a cup of cocoa and go to bed.

But Count Karlstein wanted to celebrate.

'Must be nearly time, Snivelwurst!' he said, fumbling in the pocket where his watch had been. 'Where the devil's my watch? Oh yes, that confounded vagabond smashed it to pieces. I'll see he gets an extra ten years in prison.'

The cuckoo clock on the wall said it was five minutes to midnight. Count Karlstein saw it and gulped. Even though he'd kept his bargain with Zamiel, he was still a little nervous.

'And now you're free of your terrible burden, Your Splenditude, what are you going to do?' said Snivelwurst.

As he stood there feeling pleased with himself, Count Karlstein heard something that he didn't want to hear.

He wiggled his finger in his ear, and swallowed some more brandy, and banged his head with the heel of his hand, but the sound was still there, and getting louder, too.

'Can you hear that, Snivelwurst?' he said.

'Hear what, Your Bountifulness?'

'That – out there —'

Count Karlstein ran to the window and snatched the curtain aside.

Count Karlstein ran from place to place, trying to hide. He tried to hide behind the tapestry, but his knocking knees gave him away. He tried to hide in the wastepaper basket, but it was too small. He tried to hide in the desk drawer, but Snivelwurst had got there before him. He tried to hide under the bearskin rug, but it kept shrugging itself off and left him bare too. If the cuckoo clock hadn't been full of cuckoo, he'd have tried to get into that.

83

But it was no good. As the last cuckoo sounded, he fell to his trembling knees.

'Oh, oh, oh! What's going to happen? I feel terrible! I feel as if I'm burning – I feel cold all over – I'm frightened – help! Help!'

But the terrible sounds got louder and louder.

'No! No!' cried Count Karlstein. 'I'm sorry! It was a joke! I'll be good!'

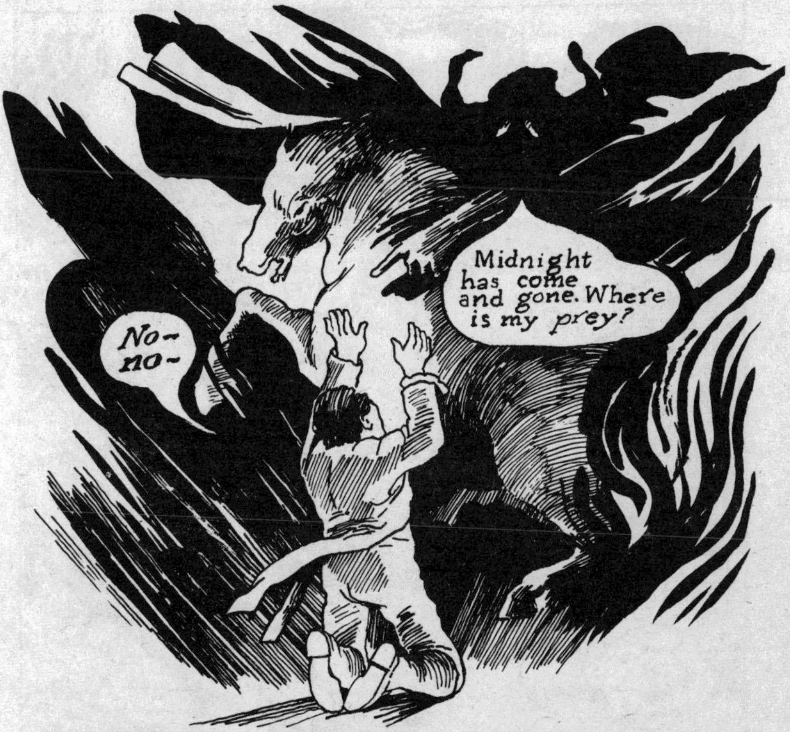
No-no-
Midnight has come and gone. Where is my *prey?*

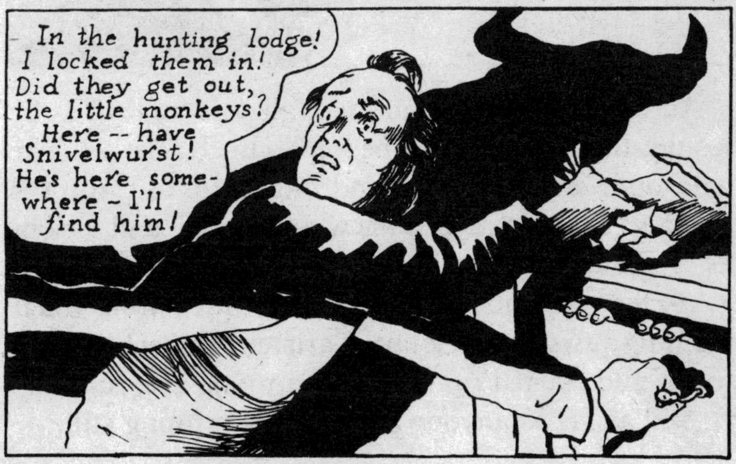
In the hunting lodge! I locked them in! Did they get out, the little monkeys? Here -- have Snivelwurst! He's here somewhere - I'll *find* him!

And cringe and beg and wriggle and squirm as he would, there was no escape for Count Karlstein. The wild hunt swept him up and flung him out into the sky; and Zamiel cracked his whip, as long and vicious as a streak of lightning, and the phantom hounds gave tongue and slavered luminously from their foaming jaws, and Count Karlstein screeched with terror and started running and running and running.

And as far as anyone knows, he's running still.

CHAPTER EIGHT
Marksmanship, or
The Broken Coin

Next morning, the sun came out early. Birds were singing, the river was splashing away to itself, and the snow sparkled on the platform where the Burgomaster and the Corporation were going to preside over the shooting contest. The whole village was getting ready.

Herr Pistlpacker, the referee, was setting up the target when four bedraggled figures came wandering on to the village green.

But Max had had almost enough of muskets. And there was something else on his mind, anyway.

'It's these britches,' he said. 'I can't go about looking like this, I'll get arrested again. Me and the master's luggage is still in the Jolly Huntsman – I'll go and see if I can find another pair. Besides, I'm blooming hungry. I reckon we could all do with some breakfast, after traipsing about all night. Come on – I'll buy us all a plate of sausages.'

That was the most difficult problem of all. Eliza said that Miss Davenport would take them in, if she ever came back, but Max said that the law would only allow them to go with relatives. It was relatives or the orphanage, he said, and he should know, being in the profession.

'Were you an orphan, Max?' said Lucy.

'Yes,' he said. 'I was brought up in the orphanage in Geneva. It weren't such a bad place. You got any cousins anywhere?'

'No,' said Charlotte. 'Only our uncle.'

But none of them knew what had happened to him. They all sat round looking mournful and feeling sorry for one another, until it was time for the shooting contest.

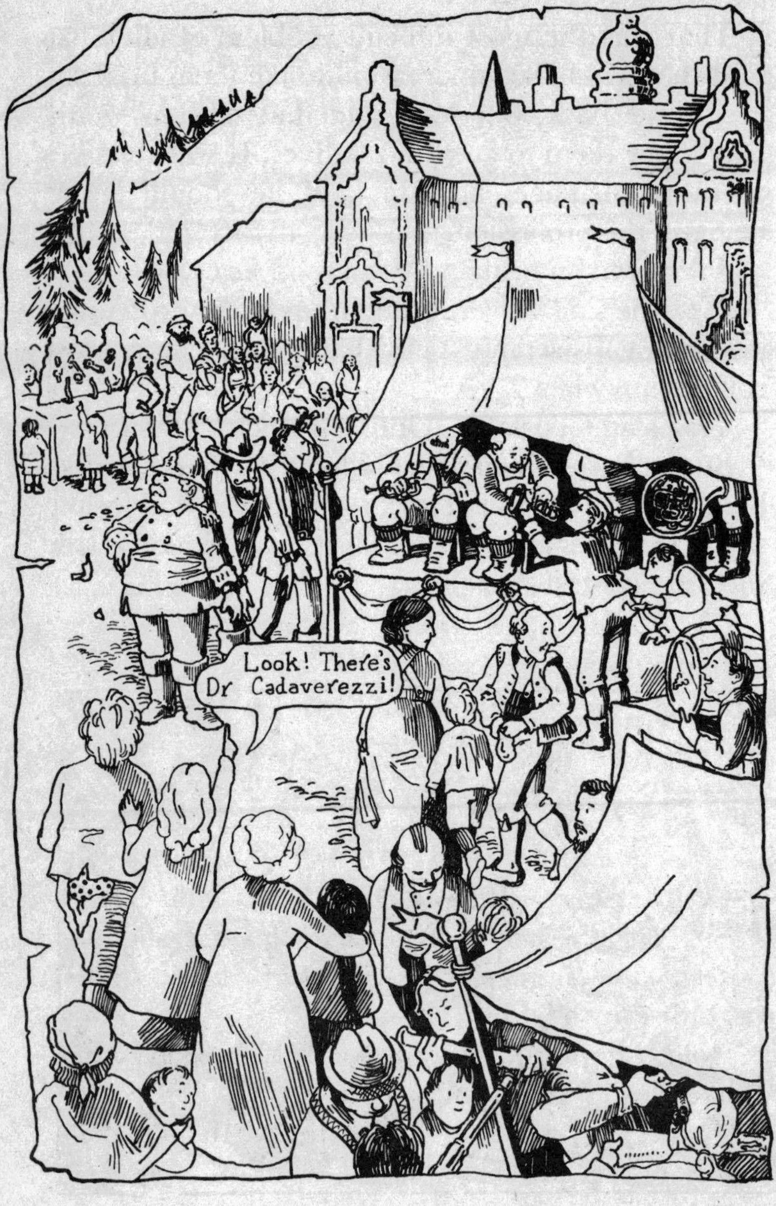
Look! There's Dr Cadaverezzi!

Sergeant Snitsch wanted to get Dr Cadaverezzi in the prison carriage straight away before he escaped again.

But Dr Cadaverezzi said, 'Sergeant, can we not stay to watch the shooting contest? After all, you might be needed to maintain law and order.'

'That's true, Sergeant,' said Constable Winkelburg nervously. 'There's a lot of strangers about . . .'

'Bosh!' said Sergeant Snitsch.

'Go on, Sergeant!' said Max.

'Yes, let him watch!' said somebody else. And 'He won't escape!' And 'Be a sport, Sergeant!'

All the people who'd enjoyed Dr Cadaverezzi's show the night before were there for the shooting contest, and Sergeant Snitsch had to agree that it was only fair to let him see it.

'Hold him tight, mind,' he said to Constable Winkelburg. 'He's as slippery as an eel.'

Then the Burgomaster stepped on to the platform, and the municipal band played a fanfare.

The referee said that Max could enter.

'But you've got to have a musket, young man,' he said.

'Ah, well, that's the problem, you see,' Max began, but he didn't get any further, because Dr Cadaverezzi spoke up.

Max took his place with the other competitors. Constable Winkelburg looked at the prisoner's pockets uneasily, wondering what else might come out of them.

Meanwhile, the referee was explaining the rules.

'Each competitor shoots in the order in which his name is drawn out of His Worship the Burgomaster's hat by Her Worshipfulness the Lady Burgomistress. One shot only, and the first to hit the target wins.'

The first competitor stepped up to shoot. And missed. Then the second, and the third, and the fourth, and they all missed, too.

'It must be harder than it looks,' said Lucy.

Her Worshipfulness the Lady Burgomistress was fumbling in His Worship the Burgomaster's hat. She took out the next piece of paper and handed it to the referee, who called out: 'Max Grindoff!'

'That's you, Maxie!' said Eliza. 'Good luck!'

Max came to the mark, looking bold and fearless. Eliza felt her heart go *twang* with pride. He lifted up the musket, put it to his shoulder, squinted along the barrel, and then took a little step sideways to get his balance.

But he'd never been lucky with muskets. When he put his foot down again, he put it on a stone. So this happened:

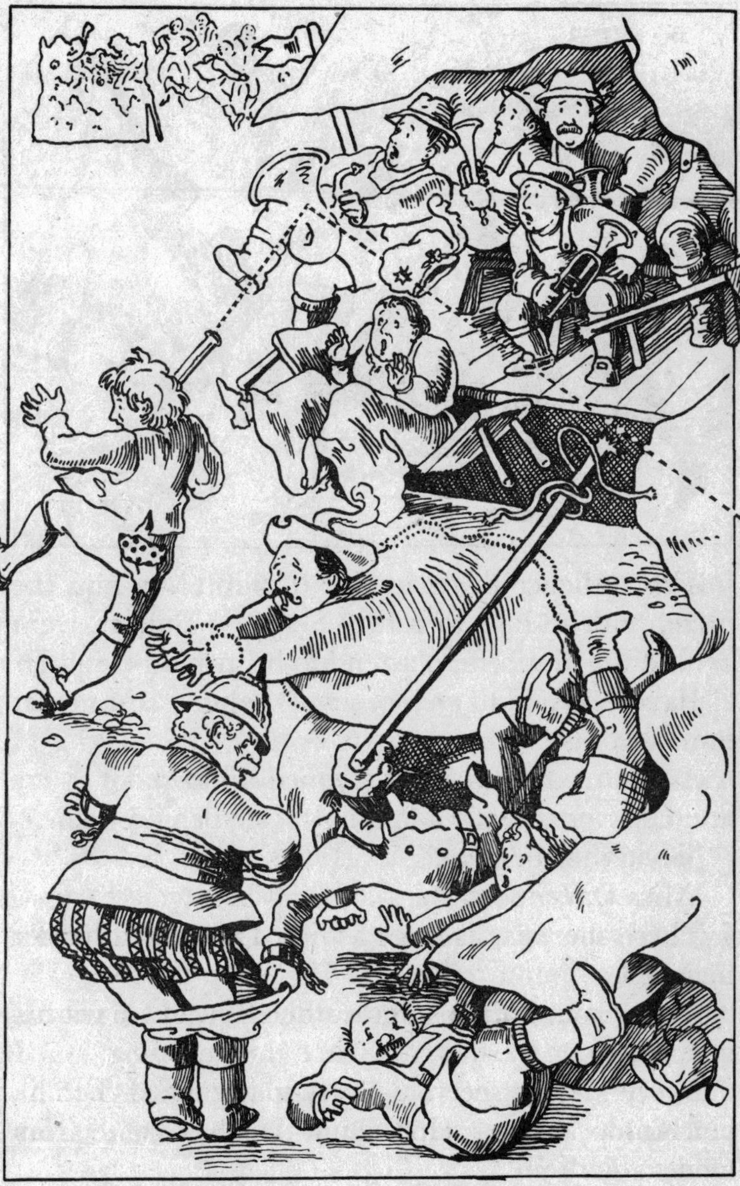

The audience loved it. But it didn't win him the prize, and he had to retire. Sergeant Snitsch went behind the platform to attend to his trousers, and Dr Cadaverezzi had to go too, since he didn't want to let him out of his sight.

As the next competitor stepped up to shoot, Lucy and Charlotte heard a familiar voice behind them.

'Good morning, girls!'

'Miss Davenport!'

There she was, as large as life. They could hardly believe it.

'Lucy, your hair is still disordered. And Charlotte, you have not washed your face this morning. But I am very glad to see you – very glad indeed. I think you know Meister Hoffmann? He has come from Geneva with me.'

The old lawyer bowed to them both, and they curtseyed to him.

They didn't have time to ask any questions, because the Burgomaster and his Worshipful wife had struggled out of the canvas by now, and the referee was looking at the next piece of paper.

'Peter Kelmar!' he called out.

There was a cheer as Peter appeared. Lucy and Charlotte cheered louder than anyone. He stepped up to the mark and took aim, but —

The Sergeant got out of the way, grumbling. He'd left Constable Winkelburg chained to Dr Cadaverezzi behind the platform, and the poor old man was quaking in his boots. But the Doctor was as good as gold for once, watching the contest with everyone else.

Peter lifted the musket to his shoulder and took aim at the target. The barrel was as steady as a rock. Slowly he squeezed the trigger and —

The audience thought that was even better than Max's shot. They laughed and cheered and roared. His Worship the Burgomaster presented Peter with a bag of gold and a Forest Ranger's hat, and everyone started thinking about lunch.

But then Miss Davenport climbed up on to the platform and clapped her hands. Silence fell.

'Your Worship, ladies and gentlemen,' she said. 'I have a sombre announcement to make. Heinrich Müller, Count Karlstein, is no more.'

'No more what?' said Max, but Miss Davenport frowned majestically at him, and he shut up.

'As this concerns the whole village,' she went on, 'it needs to be dealt with straight away. I call to witness the celebrated lawyer, Meister Hoffmann.'

The lawyer came to the platform. Everyone was quiet, waiting to hear what he was going to say.

'The question of the Karlstein estate is a very unusual one,' he began. 'First, there are his two nieces – Miss Lucy and Miss Charlotte.'

'As these two young ladies are without living relatives,' the old lawyer went on, 'they are declared wards of court, and taken into custody.'

'You'll be all right,' said Max. 'I could tell you some tales —'

'Quiet, please!' said the lawyer sternly. 'However, there is a complication. The late Count Karlstein had no claim to the estate!'

That caused a sensation. People all burst out talking at once; they'd never heard anything like it.

'What's that mean?' whispered Max to Lucy.

'It means he wasn't really Count Karlstein! Oh, I don't know what it means! Listen!'

Eliza was wriggling as if a beetle had got down her dress. She was making little squeaking noises, too, and people nearby thought she'd gone mad.

But then she found what she was looking for.

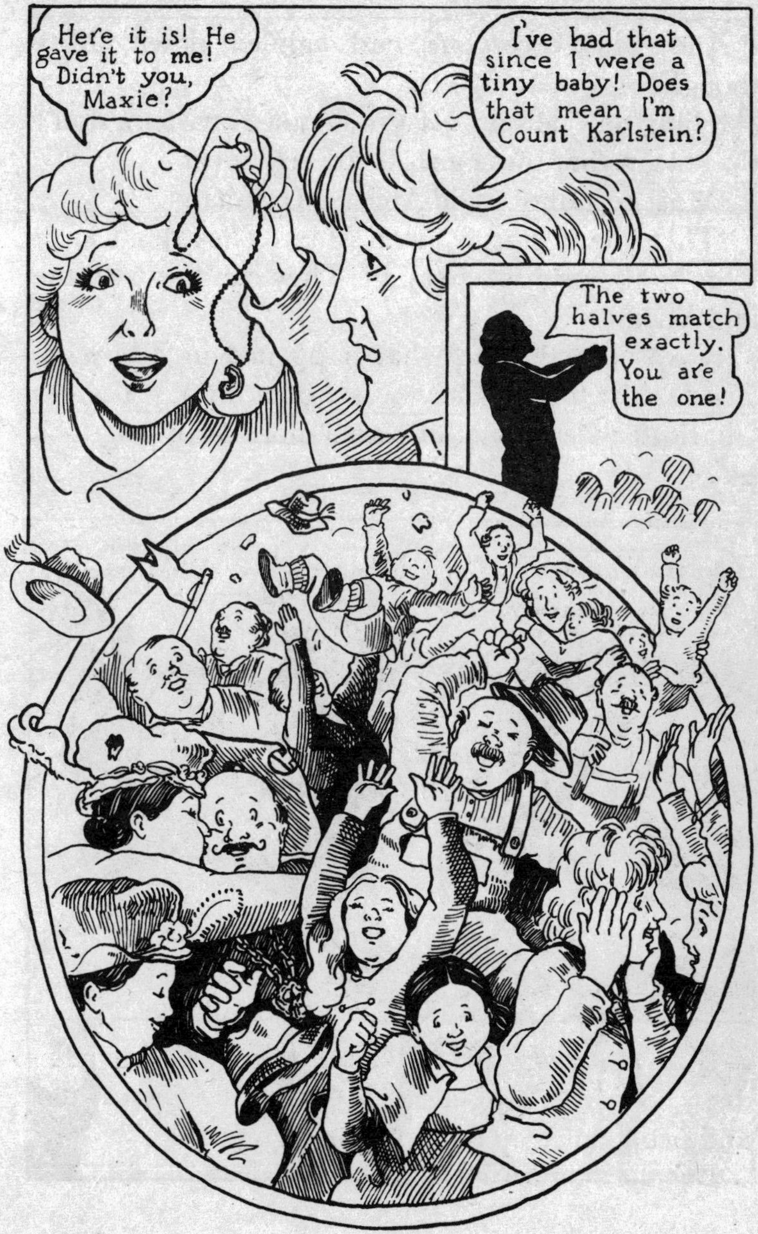
Here it is! He gave it to me! Didn't you, Maxie?
I've had that since I were a tiny baby! Does that mean I'm Count Karlstein?
The two halves match exactly. You are the one!

And when everyone had calmed down, Max thought of something else.

'Hang on,' he said. 'If I'm Count Karlstein, don't that mean that these girls is my relations?'

'Most certainly,' said Meister Hoffmann.

'Then that's simple,' said Max. 'They don't have to go to the orphanage at all. They can live with me and Eliza!'

It was exactly like what happened in *Adeline, or The Skeleton Bride*. Lucy was about to say that to Charlotte when something even more surprising took place.

CHAPTER NINE
Euphoria, or
The Huntsman's Polka

Well, that surprised everyone.

'I was going to escape later on anyway,' Dr Cadaverezzi explained, 'but now I don't have to. Miss Davenport!' he went on, bowing very deeply, 'I have been seeking you for many months – ever since our paths were separated long ago . . .'

Miss Davenport blushed, and the two of them wandered down to the river to hold hands and things. Max was kissing Eliza, Peter was trying on his Forest Ranger's hat, and Her Worshipfulness the Lady Burgomistress was talking to Lucy and Charlotte. The Karlstein Silver Band struck up a jolly tune called 'The Huntsman's Polka' and soon everyone was dancing, even Sergeant Snitsch.

Constable Winkelburg didn't want to dance, because his feet were hurting, so he had some beer and sausages instead.

And that's the end of the story.

But on winter nights when the moon is high and the clouds race across it like a pack of hungry wolves, you can hear faint echoes of a hunting horn over the mountains. And on All Souls' Eve every house is shut, every door bolted, and every fireside is ringed with wide-eyed faces, listening to the tale of the Prince of the Forest, the Dark Hunter, the Demon Zamiel.

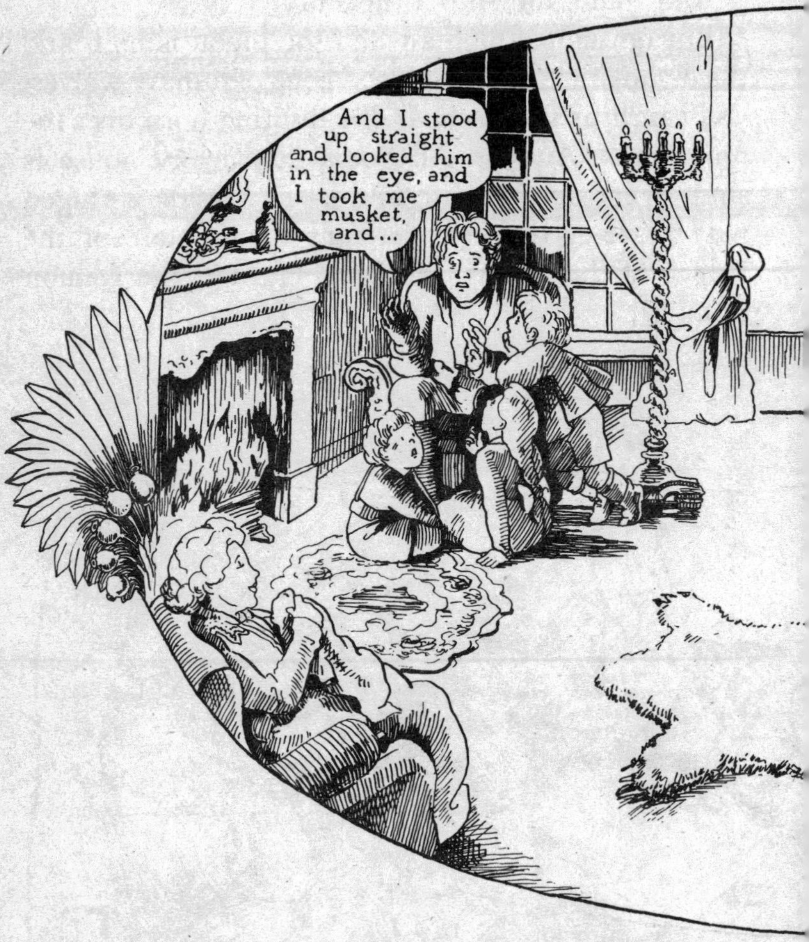
And I stood up straight and looked him in the eye, and I took me musket, and...

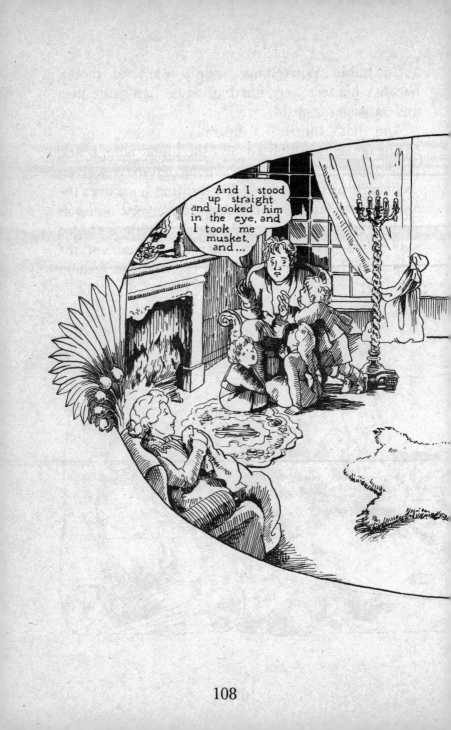

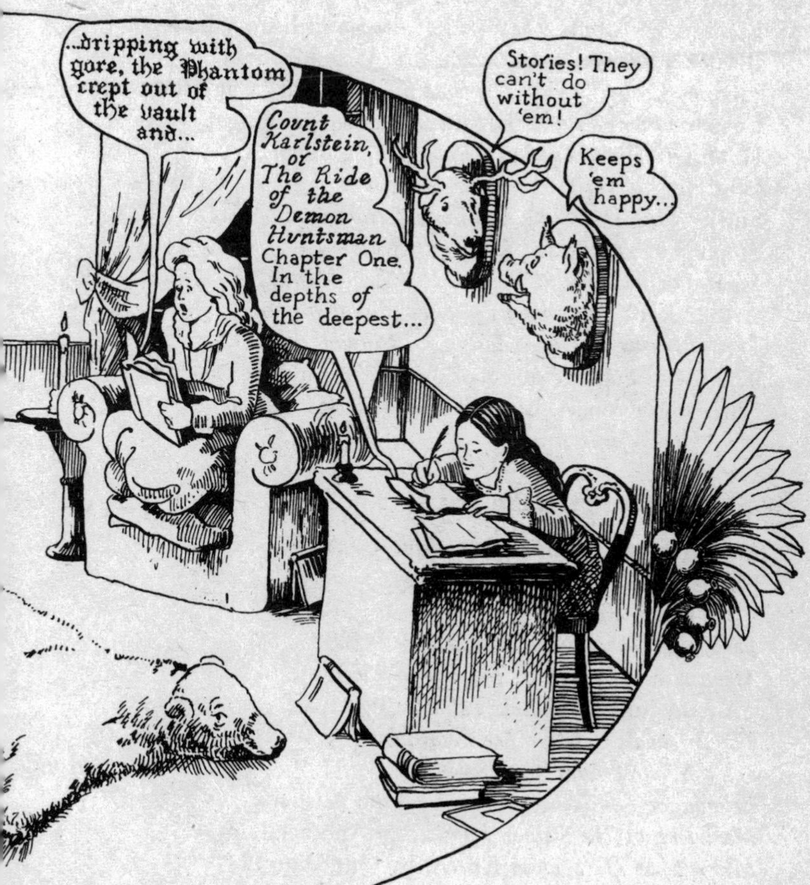
...dripping with gore, the Phantom crept out of the vault and...
Count Karlstein, or The Ride of the Demon Huntsman Chapter One. In the depths of the deepest...
Stories! They can't do without 'em!
Keeps 'em happy...

Works consulted and ideas stolen from:

Janet and Allan Ahlberg, *The Jolly Postman or Other People's Letters* (a picture book)
Brian W. Aldiss, *The Malacia Tapestry* (a novel)
Richard D. Altick, *The Shows of London* (a history book)
Baedeker's *Guide to the Eastern Alps* (a guidebook)
Jacques Louis David, *The Oath of the Horatii* (a painting)
Caspar David Friedrich, *various pictures* (paintings)
Hammer Films, *The Devil Rides Out* (a film)
Will Hay, *Ask a Policeman* (a film)
Shirley Hughes, *Chips and Jessie* (a picture book)
Stephen Leacock, *The Conjurer's Revenge* (a short story)
Isaac Pocock, *The Miller and His Men* (a play)
Arthur Rackham, *various pictures* (illustrations)
Percy Bysshe Shelley, *Zastrozzi* (a novel)
The Swiss Police Handbook (a police handbook)
Carl Maria von Weber, *Der Freischütz* (an opera)

Works referred to in the text:

Amelia, or The Phantom of the Vault, by A Lady
Rudolph, or The Hermit of the Forest,
    by David Fickling
Verezzi, or The Poisoned Chalice, by P.B.S.
Montoni the Vampyre, or The Cup of Blood,
    by the author of *Pixie Tales for Wee Folks*
The Brigand's Cave, or The Fatal Marriage,
    by A Governess
Belinda, or The Skeleton Crew, by Jane Austen
Marianna, or The Sicilian Captive, by Another Lady
Miranda, or The Spanish Heiress, by One Who Is
    Almost A Lady
Emilia, or The Pedlar's Bequest, by the author of
    Tough Guys Shoot First
Adeline, or The Skeleton Bride, by Mrs Beeton
Valloni, or The Spectre of the Lake, by Annie Eaton

ADVERTISEMENT

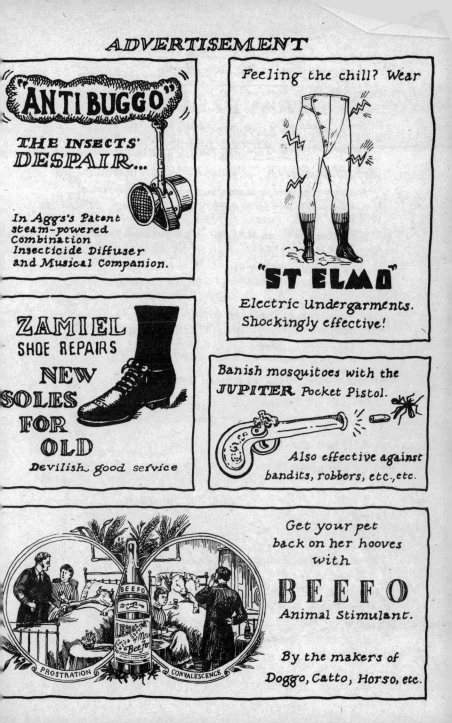

"ANTI BUGGO"

THE INSECTS' DESPAIR...

In Aggs's Patent steam-powered Combination Insecticide Diffuser and Musical Companion.

Feeling the chill? Wear

"ST ELMO"

Electric Undergarments. Shockingly effective!

ZAMIEL
SHOE REPAIRS
NEW SOLES FOR OLD

Devilish good service

Banish mosquitoes with the **JUPITER** Pocket Pistol.

Also effective against bandits, robbers, etc., etc.

PROSTRATION   CONVALESCENCE

Get your pet back on her hooves with

BEEFO
Animal Stimulant.

By the makers of Doggo, Catto, Horso, etc.

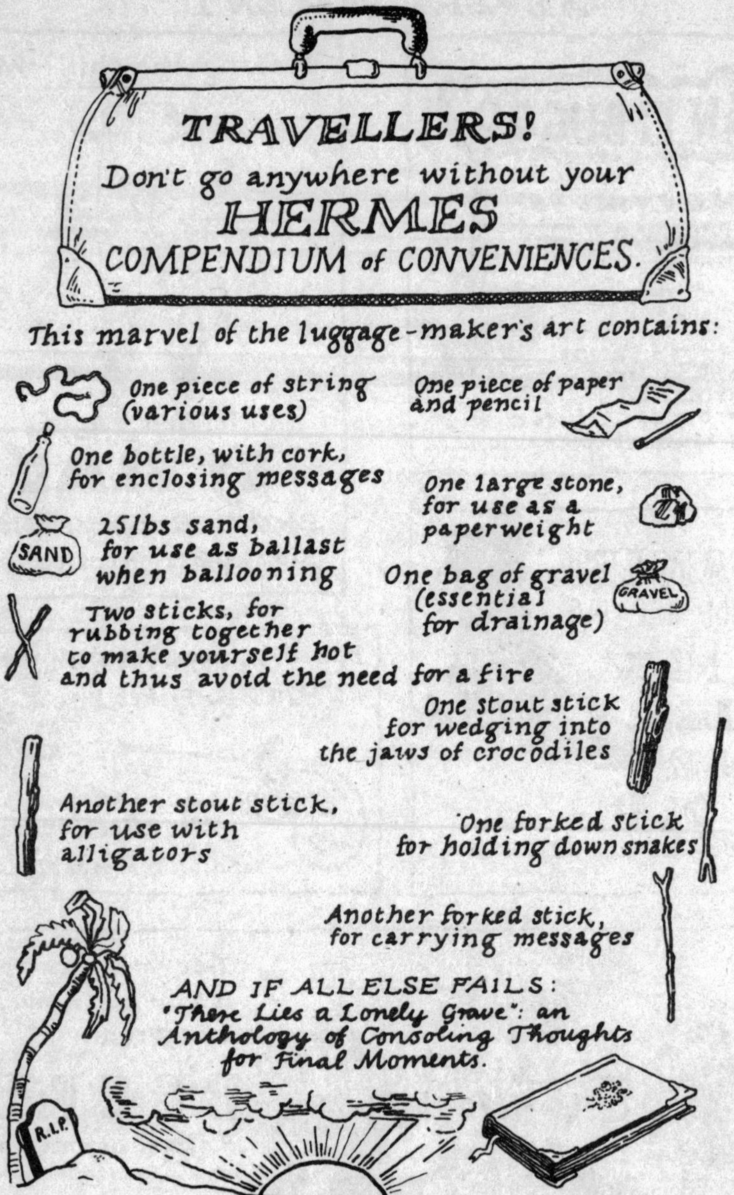
TRAVELLERS!
Don't go anywhere without your
HERMES
COMPENDIUM of CONVENIENCES.
This marvel of the luggage-maker's art contains:
One piece of string (various uses)
One piece of paper and pencil
One bottle, with cork, for enclosing messages
One large stone, for use as a paperweight
25lbs sand, for use as ballast when ballooning
SAND
One bag of gravel (essential for drainage)
GRAVEL
Two sticks, for rubbing together to make yourself hot and thus avoid the need for a fire
One stout stick for wedging into the jaws of crocodiles
Another stout stick, for use with alligators
One forked stick for holding down snakes
Another forked stick, for carrying messages
AND IF ALL ELSE FAILS:
"There Lies a Lonely Grave": an Anthology of Consoling Thoughts for Final Moments.
R.I.P.